Dragon's Day

by Liza Charlesworth

ISBN: 978-1-338-78274-5
Illustrated by Roger Simó
Copyright © 2021 by Liza Charlesworth. All rights reserved.
Published by Scholastic Inc., 557 Broadway, New York, NY 10012

10 9 8 7 6 5 4 3 2 1   68   21 22 23 24 25 26 27/0

Printed in Jiaxing, China. First printing, June 2021.

What does Dragon
want to do today?
She wants to ride!

What does Dragon
want to do today?
She wants to hide!

3

What does Dragon
want to do today?
She wants to bat!

What does Dragon
want to do today?
She wants to chat!

5

What does Dragon
want to do today?
She wants to rake!

What does Dragon
want to do today?
She wants to bake!

What a cake!